W9-CIG-115

Dear Parent:

Congratulations! Your child is taking the first steps on an exciting journey. The destination? Independent reading!

STEP INTO READING® will help your child get there. The program offers five steps to reading success. Each step includes fun stories and colorful art. There are also Step into Reading Sticker Books, Step into Reading Math Readers, Step into Reading Write-In Readers, Step into Reading Phonics Readers, and Step into Reading Phonics First Steps! Boxed Sets—a complete literacy program with something for every child.

Learning to Read, Step by Step!

Ready to Read   Preschool–Kindergarten
• big type and easy words • rhyme and rhythm • picture clues
For children who know the alphabet and are eager to begin reading.

Reading with Help   Preschool–Grade 1
• basic vocabulary • short sentences • simple stories
For children who recognize familiar words and sound out new words with help.

Reading on Your Own   Grades 1–3
• engaging characters • easy-to-follow plots • popular topics
For children who are ready to read on their own.

Reading Paragraphs   Grades 2–3
• challenging vocabulary • short paragraphs • exciting stories
For newly independent readers who read simple sentences with confidence.

Ready for Chapters   Grades 2–4
• chapters • longer paragraphs • full-color art
For children who want to take the plunge into chapter books but still like colorful pictures.

STEP INTO READING® is designed to give every child a successful reading experience. The grade levels are only guides. Children can progress through the steps at their own speed, developing confidence in their reading, no matter what their grade.

Remember, a lifetime love of reading starts with a single step!

For Tammy, my MOH
— M.L.

www.stepintoreading.com
www.randomhouse.com/kids/disney

Educators and librarians, for a variety of teaching tools, visit us at
www.randomhouse.com/teachers

Library of Congress Cataloging-in-Publication Data
Lagonegro, Melissa.
A dream for a princess / by Melissa Lagonegro.
    p. cm. — (Step into reading. A Step 2 book)
SUMMARY: Simplified retelling of the tale of Cinderella, a kitchen maid mistreated by her stepmother and stepsisters who, with the help of her fairy godmother, attends the palace ball and meets the prince of her dreams.
ISBN 0-7364-2340-0 (trade) — ISBN 0-7364-8044-7 (lib. bdg.)
[1. Fairy tales. 2. Folklore—France.] I. Cinderella. English. II. Title. III. Series: Step into reading. Step 2 book.
PZ8.L1362Dr 2005 398.2'0944'02—dc22   2004020981

Printed in the United States of America   10 9 8 7 6 5 4 3 2 1

STEP INTO READING®

STEP 2

DISNEY
◆PRINCESS

A Dream for a Princess

By Melissa Lagonegro

Illustrated by Pulsar Estudio

Random House 🏠 New York

There once was a girl
named Cinderella.
She was kind and gentle.

Cinderella lived with
her wicked Stepmother
and stepsisters.

She had many chores.

She served them tea.

She cooked their food.

She washed their clothes.

"Get my scarf!"

yelled one sister.

"Fix my dress!"

shouted the other.

They were very mean
to poor Cinderella.

One day,
a letter came
from the palace.
"Come meet the Prince
at a Royal Ball," it said.

The stepsisters
were very excited.
Cinderella was, too!

Cinderella dreamed of
wearing a fancy gown . . .

. . . and dancing with
the Prince.

Cinderella's Stepmother
gave her more chores.
Cinderella did not
have time to make
her ball gown.

"Surprise!"
cried her little friends.
They had made her
a fancy gown.

"Now I can go
to the ball!"
cheered Cinderella.

Oh, no!
The stepsisters
tore her gown.
It was ruined!

Cinderella cried.

Piff, puff, poof!

Her Fairy Godmother

appeared.

"You cannot go
to the ball
like that," she said.

She waved
her magic wand.
<u>Poof!</u>

A royal coach.

White horses.

Two coachmen.

And a beautiful gown!

Cinderella was headed
to the ball!

At the ball,
the Prince saw
Cinderella.

"May I have this dance?" he asked.

They danced . . .

. . . and danced . . .

. . . and danced.

Cinderella was so happy.
She was wearing
a fancy gown.

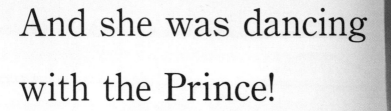

And she was dancing
with the Prince!

Her dream had come true!